T0157422

EVERYONE'S PERSPECTIVE

Order this book online at www.trafford.com/07-2608
or email orders@trafford.com

Most Trafford titles are also available at major online book retailers.

© Copyright 2009 Stephnie Morgan.
All rights reserved. No part of this publication may be reproduced, stored in a retrieval
system, or transmitted, in any form or by any means, electronic, mechanical, photocopying,
recording, or otherwise, without the written prior permission of the author.

Printed in Victoria, BC, Canada.

ISBN: 978-1-4251-5790-6 (sc)

ISBN: 978-1-4251-7970-0 (e)

*Our mission is to efficiently provide the world's finest, most comprehensive
book publishing service, enabling every author to experience success.
To find out how to publish your book, your way, and have it available
worldwide, visit us online at www.trafford.com/10510*

 www.trafford.com

North America & international
toll-free: 1 888 232 4444 (USA & Canada)
phone: 250 383 6864 ♦ fax: 812 355 4082

EVERYONE'S PERSPECTIVE

Simon Eliot:

Simon Eliot was a boy of seventeen. He had shoulder length limp straight black hair that he hardly attempted to comb and fell across his face loosely hiding his equally dark eyes as well as the rest of his face. His thin pale pink lips locked tightly together as he hardly attempted to smile, and his face always bore the same scowling countenance without a doubt or fail.

He was a tall boy of five foot eight but slouched whenever possible, and he walked as though he was dragging his feet and sometimes really was. All this though he couldn't help and only he, he thought, knew why. For years he had been neglected by the one whom he thought should have loved him best, and months of decay due to various toxic drug use saw Simon falling deeper into obscurity and finally losing his way.

He lived with his unsuspecting family in a quiet residential area in Surrey. Their house was big and elaborate and had a lot of garden space; their driveway could hold two cars parked side by side, and there was still a sufficient enough pathway for them all to trot out of the house. Everything seemed perfect.

His mother, Suzie, took pride in the house making sure everything was immaculate and always in its place, whilst his father worked long hours to provide for the family. His sister, Eleanor, who was also his twin, spent most of her time with her friends. Always out and having fun, she seemed the most unsuspecting of them all.

Simon attended Lake Hill Grammar School as well as his sister, and although she could be seen conversing with many of the other pupils, Simon was always by himself. And just like his sister, when she was at home, he'd lock himself into his room - but not for the same purposes.

EVERYONE'S PERSPECTIVE

Simon is mother:

'I spend most of my time in my room. It's easier there. I don't have to deal with my mother trying to fix everything all the time whilst all the while ignoring the true members of this family - not the stupid neighbour who she spends every waking minute of the day trying to impress. Trying to pretend that she is the dutiful wife and mother and everything is fine. It is NOT! My only escape from her annoying need to fix everything is to destroy something. Myself.

'The drugs help me to escape from her superficial act. She never notices me when I speak. When I try to have a one to one with her she's too busy tidying up. If she knew I had a drug problem she'd probably want to trade me in for a newer more acceptable son who wasn't a disappointment to her. It's better to be high for a short while than low all the time.'

Simon would witness his mother on his way to school busying herself in the kitchen. Her long turquoise silk nightgown practically trailing on the floor, and if it wasn't for her high heeled turquoise slippers, it probably would have been. Humming to herself as she turned on the cooker, preparing dinner at breakfast time, she wouldn't even hear her vulnerable only son say 'Bye' as he left the house.

He'd slam the door on his departure hoping that she would acknowledge him, but on his look back, he not only saw, but heard his mother singing out loud jubilantly as though nothing had happened. Simon's face would contort in anger as he turned and walk away.

'I can't even think of one thing I like about her, she gives me so many reasons to hate her, I could stand in front of her quite literally a blazed and she still would look right through me. Hear a pin drop as I screamed on the top of my lungs. Why should she care?

'The only way how she would even look at me, is if her precious neighbours were around and I sat sullen. Then she'd stare at me right in the eyes, her eyes blazed with controlled reproof.'

4
EVERYONE'S PERSPECTIVE

Simon on his father:

'My father spends most of his time at work. It's been like that for a while now. Can't remember the last time he's had a full day in the house. He even works on the weekend and never really takes breaks, so I hardly get to see him.

'I love my father. Well … he's easier to cope with than my mother, anyway. At least he'll acknowledge my presence sometimes, at least until my mother shows up. But she's always there, so it's just fleeting moments when we walk past each other and he'll rub his hand in my hair and mess it up. A broad grin will splash across his face as I look up, and even I can't help but smile back. But then mum will make her entrance and the mood will change.

'My father's really cool though. When I was younger we use to go to the park: him, Elle and me - mother would spend her time at home - and we would play football, but not in the competitive sense, we'd just all chase the ball and whoever got there first would give it one vicious kick and it'd just end up anywhere. They were good times.

'We seemed really close back then: the three of us. But I suppose that is the problem: it's always been just the three of us; She had better things to do with her time than play games with us.

'Then dad started working a lot more. So Elle and I would see him less. Mother wanted there to be a bigger income to make the house a lot more elaborate. The more money dad made, the more she could show off to the neighbours. They seem to have some sort of futile competition amongst themselves.

'Maybe if she did some of the work for a change, and she was the one grafting, dad and I would be closer, and me and Elle more like brother and sister; we all seem like distant strangers living under the same roof. None of us seem to talk to each other anymore.

'My father knows nothing of my drug use. Don't think there's

EVERYONE'S PERSPECTIVE

anything that anyone can do about it now anyway. I think I've gone too far.

'I started off with just the occasional headache tablets - but at the time I did have a headache, so nothing wrong there. But then my father started spending more and more time at work, and Elle would always be out with her multitude of friends, and of course mother and I wouldn't even talk to each other - or she wouldn't talk to me. I became distant with everyone and just shut myself into my room. I hated feeling so lonely, so started taking the pills - headache tablets - to try and block things out, but they weren't strong enough.

'I raided my mother's cupboard in the bathroom and found her sleeping pills. It did the trick for a while; under the right dosage I'd sleep for hours at a time, even wake up late for school and be too drowsy in class to concentrate, which meant that my grades started to suffer. But it was absolute bliss because then I started taking acid pills. I was completely numb to everything. Would "black out" sometimes and not know where I was. Took me a while to realize I was on my bedroom floor. Anyway, I stopped hanging out with my friends because they thought I was getting a bit weird. But who needs them anyway?

'I don't know if things are better are worse since I started taking the pills. My mother still doesn't acknowledge me, my father's still cooped up at work and my sister still spends all her extra spare time with all her friends. Nothing's really changed for them. They still all act the same. But at least now I don't have to be reminded of my lonely existence.

'Dad still pats my head when he sees me, the same broad grin spread across his face. But now when I see him I smile mechanically, I already know how he'll look at me whenever he sees me and as long as I smile back and pretend to smile with some affection, he is non the wiser.

'I've become really good at faking feelings that are no longer there. I even surprise myself.'

Simon on his sister:

EVERYONE'S PERSPECTIVE

'I think my sister's completely clueless to what's going on. Though lately, she has been looking at me strangely. When we sit around the dining table for dinner and everyone's busily eating their food, I normally just sit there picking at it.

'Dad will devour his food when he's at home. He'll eat as though he hasn't eaten in months, and that is his first serving after a painful fast. Mum will sit there eating elegantly, cutting her meat into tiny portions and savouring the taste as if the food taste better that way. But then I'll look around to Elle and I'll notices her gazing at me.

'She looks at me funny. I see it sometimes when she doesn't think I'm looking. Not just around the table but other places too. Sometimes after I stir after I've "blacked out" on the floor, my vision is blurry, but I could swear I see her outline at my door, just standing there watching me. But then I'll turn and push myself to my full height, eyes in complete focus, and when I look back nobody's there, and more to that, my door is shut. Maybe I'm just paranoid. Who knows? She never talks to me anyway. So why would she be watching me?

'It didn't use to be like this. Elle and I used to talk loads. In fact, we were inseparable. Wherever she was I was there, and wherever I was, she'd be there also. But that twin thing doesn't seem to work anymore. We no longer have a connection.

'I remember how we use to play when we were little. We use to chase each other around the garden laughing. Elle use to have a mingled shrill scream with her laugh, the kind that only children can produce. It was so precious, I use to tickle her like crazy in the house. Hours and hours we would spend by each other's side, sometimes just sitting in silence not doing anything.

'Whenever I was hurt she'd feel it with far more intensity than I would. She would cry in earnest as I sat quietly with the pain. Anyone would have thought that it was her that had cut herself or fell and grazed her knee.

EVERYONE'S PERSPECTIVE

'She was so sweet to me too; carried me drinks for the rest of the day. Sat down quietly beside me stroking my hair. Asked me occasionally if I was sure I was okay, if there was anything she could get me, that it'd be no trouble. No trouble at all.

'Sometimes, when I'm totally out of it, it's as though I can feel her presence; still feel her tender touch on my hair, still feel her warm breath against my face telling me "it'll be alright". But when I come round there's no-one there. Just me all alone in my room.

'I miss my precious sister. Sometimes I feel so alone. Forlorn and despicable! No wonder I am so wretched! How would my sister look at me now if she knew what I had become! How could she bear to look at me if she saw how much I'd maimed my mind! All I wanted was to numb the pain and now it's taken over me! I can't sleep! I can't breathe! I can't stand to look at myself when I see how haggard I've become! Oh, I miss my sister. I miss her so much! But now I have lost her console.

'I've tried to stop. I have! But the stress just takes over again. My mind won't function without them now. I've gone too far within myself.

'Sometimes I think if I could only destroy them. Flush them down the toilet or even bury them out in the field … but then I see faces coming up from the surface of the water. Leering at me. Taunting me. Laughing away uncontrollably. Telling me that nobody wants me.

'I try not to listen, but they're too strong; they mock me and tell me that I am weak. That I'm not worthy of my sister's affections. That I need them: I need the drugs. They are the only things that will love me. They will guide and protect me. They will make everything be alright. I'll never have to worry about anything as long as I have them. I'll soon never worry at all. Soon I'll be like all those they have helped before me. And I'll rest peacefully. Untroubled by another living soul.'

Simon on his school:

'I use to be really good at school. Get good grades, answer questions,

EVERYONE'S PERSPECTIVE

have my assignments in on time and still have time to spare - which I would normally spend hanging out with friends. Now I don't have or do any of those things.

'My friends and I use to be very close; hang out at lunch times eating and playing football: this was a continuation from break time. We'd sit huddled together in class. Join up in the corridors when we had different lessons. And of course, we'd all walk home together - Peter and Paul - they're brothers, and Gary. Now I see the three of them huddled up together looking over my way and turning back quickly. Sometimes Elle even seems to be with them, looking over just as they do, whispering closely together. Of course, Elle doesn't stay there long enough with them; she has other friends whom she devotes her time to. But I do find it strange how she's always with my friends, especially Paul. What do they find so interesting that they're always around each other?

'I spend all of my time alone now that my friends have all deserted me. I don't mind it, it's just a bit wearisome being somewhere with so many people and not having anyone around you. It's very tedious. I suppose I could take all that extra time to catch up on my work, because, I really need to. Apparently, I'm "destroying all my prospects", and the sensible thing to do is at least try. But every time I look at the work it seems slightly blurry and my brain instantly shuts down. It won't comply.

'It's my last year in school before I turn eighteen, then if we've done well in our exams we'll have a clear path in front of us to join the outside world. Which to everybody else means university, but to me, it means nothing.

'Careers advisors and university professors are starting to take weekly trips to my school. Each are trying to persuade the pupils to apply for their university, and the advisors are trying to set us up for the "best" jobs: how to achieve it, what we need to achieve and having the best disposition. I think I might have failed in all three':

Simon walked into his History class in the complete destruction of his

EVERYONE'S PERSPECTIVE

uniform. His red and black tie was loose, his white shirt was out, his black blazer was wide open and he was wearing trainers - which were strictly forbidden unless doing P.E. Simon clearly wasn't. His lank hair fell scruffily over his eyes and his face was some what wan. Every other pupil sitting in rows in the class - boy and girl - had the decent appearance which was required by the school: ties straight, shirts in, blazers buttoned and in the correct one inch heel flat shoes. They all stared at him on his arrival.

'You have an appointment to see a careers advisor at 9:30am.' said his history teacher: a tall skinny man with small brown eyes, thick grey hair and sunken in cheeks. He wore a black suit which seemed to rival the uniform. The deep clear voice continued. 'A university professor will also be waiting present for your appearance. If you make your way to the staff waiting room you should only be five minutes late.'

His eyes travelled from Simon's eyes pouring over his uniform, his face looked graved with disappointment.

'Please try to straighten up before you get there.' he said finally before turning back to his diligent pupils.

Simon, ignoring this, left the classroom and walked down the corridor as scruffily as he had walked in, passing notice boards, and framed certificates for perfect attendance.

As he reached the staff waiting room he could hear voices mumbling from within, one from a woman and the other from a man. He knocked the door before entering and opened the door faced with a man in a deep rich suit and a woman attired in a white straight pencil skirt and a light blue sleeveless top. Simon took a seat.

'Hello Simon,' said the woman with an outstretched hand and a broad pleasant smile baring all her teeth. 'I'm Marybeth Gold: careers advisor. How are you?'

Her voice was clear and lively, and her face looked eager. Simon, who seemed surprised, took her hand which she gripped firmly into a shake. 'I'm okay thanks.' Simon said slowly. His voice drawled and languid.

EVERYONE'S PERSPECTIVE

Seeming pretty content with this, Marybeth released his hand and pulled up to her full height. The man, who had kept himself into the background, merely looked on showing a half smile as he took in the scruffy appearance of the pupil.

'So have you thought much about what you'd like to do when you finish school?' Asked Marybeth settling into a chair besides the already seated professor.

Simon looked around before answering the question. The room had a fluffy beige carpet and the walls were painted white. It had two three-seated sofas facing each other - one of which Simon was on, and the other held the two visitors next to the door. A table holding a kettle and a microwave was pushed into the far corner, and besides that was a fridge. Turning back to the woman, Simon said 'No.'

'Oh that's okay,' she said reassuringly. 'Do you have any interests, hobbies, a favourite subject in school perhaps?'

'No.' Simon said again.

'Well … Where do you hope to be in five years time?'

'I don't know. I might be dead.' Simon said in a bored voice.

The smile on Gold's face seemed to slip a bit. She turned around to look at the man before saying in a feigned brisk voice. 'Well maybe looking at some university options and flicking through a prospectus might help? Mr Thomas here,' she indicated at the man, 'is the History professor at one of the most prestigious universities in England, perhaps you'd like to take a quick look through one of the prospectus?'

Simon shook his head as he gazed up at the ceiling. Gold and Thomas exchanged disapproving looks. And Simon left the room the same as he had entered; empty handed and dishevelled.

Suzie Eliot:

Suzie Eliot stood in the kitchen humming to herself as she arranged some orange and red tulips in a vase. She was a woman of thirty-seven and

EVERYONE'S PERSPECTIVE

since the age of eighteen had set up home with her computer consultant husband Charles. As Charles worked long hours Suzie took to tending to the home. And from the age of twenty, after the birth of their twin son and daughter, found herself occupied with two small children and a house to deal with all by herself. Suzie started preoccupying her time with the well being of the house obsessively as a way of distracting herself.

She had thick bouncy shoulder-length black hair, dark brown eyes and thin pale pink lips, which always curled into a half smile which gave her a pleasant complacent countenance. She was tall and thin but healthy looking, and took great pride in her appearance, second to the house.

The house was spotlessly clean. Vases with vibrant coloured flowers were placed in every room. Plates organized by colour were laid onto shelves. Glasses and cups were organized by size and laid out onto shelves adjacent to those. The kitchen sink sparkled clean; not a dirty dish, cup or cloth in sight. The dining table was all laid and ready as she perched the now tidied and beautifully arranged flowers in their vase in the centre.

The living room's sofa and chairs all held their own individual cushions. The coffee table, with all it's lustre, held all it's sparkling silver coasters. Suzie took a seat as delicately as she could and admired her freshly clean house. It was 9am in the morning.

Suzie on her husband:

'My husband and I met when we were both in college. Both seventeen and so young and innocent. He was studying I.T and business Studies - which is what he went on to study in University. I was studying Design and Technology; I wanted to be an interior designer. Hmm! Well that didn't quite work out.

'I got myself a job at eighteen to help pay for my tuition fees. God only knows how much I hated it! But I was going to be what I was going to be. Charlie and I both started the university of our choice at eighteen.

EVERYONE'S PERSPECTIVE

It was hard, what with me working in my spare hours and studying with the others, and Charlie studying around the clock. But we made it work.

'At the weekends when there were hardly any catching up for me to do, I would leave the restaurant after my shift and go over to Charlie's parents' house. It was more like a manor really; monstrous and majestically designed. Iron gates tantalizingly withholding entrance. It was like nothing I've ever seen before!

'Well Charlie and I would spend our weekends in that house, all alone - his parents absent taking business trips or vacations. The house was ours to do as we please until Charlie and I got a place of our own a couple of months down the line. Two years just the two of us until things suddenly changed.

'I fell pregnant just a year before completing my degree and the money that I worked could no longer cover my tuition fees since getting myself in that mess! I had to quit my job. Quit university. Give up on my dream. Charlie continued his studies. He wasn't poor and working class like me. He said he would take care of me. Take care of us all. He wasn't even angry or disappointed. But I felt what he should have.

'I was disgusted with myself! So close to getting what I wanted and then watching it desert me. My life was ruined! Charlie could go ahead and do as he pleased. Spend time with his friends. Finish his degree. Accomplish all his dreams. I was stuck with two children. Trapped in my own misery.

'It's a good thing that he's successful. One of us has to be! It blights some of the pain I feel inside for my own stupid mistake. He loves the children. I can see that. He doesn't regret them at all. I wish I could feel the same way. But at least I don't regret him.

'I loved him just a mere month in our relationship and it hasn't stopped since. He's always been so kind and gentle. Always so supportive. Most men would have just made empty promises; say what they'd expect you'd want to hear and leave you when it gets too much. Not my Charlie. He's been true since day one.'

EVERYONE'S PERSPECTIVE

Suzie on her daughter:

'Despite the grave disappointment within myself. I've never regretted Eleanor. So sweet, so caring, so clever sometimes it kills me. She's always been so pure of heart. So free of spirit. So much more disciplined when it counts, not like I was. My deepest admirations goes towards my precious daughter.

'She was born first. Five minutes in fact. And from the moment I held her I loved her with all my heart.

'I used to watch her play with building blocks when she was smaller: building a huge tower then knocking it all down. She was so adorable! And at night time when I tucked her up in bed, sung her a lullaby, read her a story, she'd look up at me with her big brown eyes and smile the most precious smile I've ever seen.

'She's practically a woman now. Seventeen years old. Wow! Just one more year before finishing school then she'll be off to university experiencing to the full degree all of the things I did and some that I inevitably missed. I am so proud of her. I expect big things from her. She shouldn't let her talents go to waste.

'As far as I know she doesn't have a boyfriend and I think it's better that way. She doesn't need a man coming between her and her studies. There's plenty of time for that later: after she's accomplished her dreams.

'She was never like typical girls who dreamt about their Prince Charming. And she's never once spoken to me about a guy. She's always been too immersed in her books. The only thing she seemed to care about other than her books was her brother. I suppose it is because they're twins.

'She used to follow him around everywhere that he went. And he would do the same. Wherever there was one, there was the other. So if I ever wanted to find Eleanor, I just had to find her brother. Completely

EVERYONE'S PERSPECTIVE

inseparable.

'I never liked the way how she used to follow him around. Tailing behind him. Following his lead. She was just too close to him. I'm glad it's not like that anymore. Even if it means her hardly being in the house or shut up in her room.

'Over the years she's been spending a lot of time out with her friends. But I suppose a girl like her; as bright and as sociable as she is, cannot be expected to be a loner. She should enjoy her life. Make the best of the friends she has, unlike some.

'The only thing is ... even though she still makes time for her friends, she's also been spending a lot more time than usual in her room, especially when that brother of hers is in. She'll disappear to her room and stay there for hours - I'm sure her school work doesn't take that long.

'It's as though she has reverted to her childhood days of being her brother's henchman. When he disappears up to his room, within ten minutes she'll disappear upstairs also. I don't hear her go into her room straight away. It's as though she hovers on the landing for a while, inert or otherwise just ... lingering. Then she'll go into her room - I'll hear it after a while, and stay locked away for the remainder of the day. I don't like it; it seems very suspicious.

'Of course, I'm the only one that notices this. Her father doesn't notice a thing! But he works long hours, so I suppose he's tired. I don't want her to become a recluse like her brother; she's too good for that. She can go far. If only I could get to the bottom of her strange behaviour. If only I knew what she was doing!

'I'm not proud of myself. But sometimes when she's away at school or out with her friends, I do take the occasional peep through her room. But nothing ever seems to be out of place or out of context. I've even searched her room to see if she might have a diary. Just so I can get a better insight. Under her pillows, under her mattress, through her books, on her shelf, into her cupboards, in her wardrobe. I've even looked through her computer files to see if I can find anything. But there is nothing! I just don't understand it.'

Suzie on her son:

'Well, unlike Eleanor, I could rarely stand my son. He never did anything wrong of course, how could he? He was just a baby. But it was very clear to me that I just couldn't stand him.

'Most people and doctors would probably say that it was apparently post-natal-depression. But it was obvious to me. ME! That it certainly was NOT post-natal-depression. I loved Eleanor from the go. The precious sweet creature. But HIM. I really could not tolerate him. It was nothing to do with not having a bond, and not being able to bond with my baby. I just never liked him. That's all.

'I suppose it could be compared to a person who you've never met, but everyone tells you how much you'll love them. But as soon as you see that person, no matter how much praise they've acquired from other people, you just know that you don't like them. And there is nothing that can be said or done to change that. It's just fact.

'Simon equally had his moments of playing with the building blocks when he was small. I used to see him building one huge tower, and I must admit, he had a lot more patience than Eleanor. He'd look at the tower - a look of complacency on his face - before knocking it down, like he could actually understand and appreciate what he had done. But I never had the patience to congratulate him.

'And when he used to fall over and graze himself, he would cry and hold his hands up outstretched up to me, expecting me to pick him up, to console him. I just really couldn't. It turned my stomach. He soon stopped crying when he hurt himself. Just sit there, almost peacefully, as though he felt no pain whilst his sister did the job that I wouldn't. Felt the pain that I could not. She was like the mother that I couldn't be. Tending to the child with so much love.

EVERYONE'S PERSPECTIVE

'I never showed him any affection from the first. When I used to pick him up to put him to bed, he would rap his little hands around me and press his head on my shoulder, stroking the soft fabric of my blouse. I couldn't wait to put him down! And then when I did he'd look up at me; his big brown eyes meeting mine, a gentle smile up on his face. And then I couldn't wait to leave the room.

'He grew up pleasant enough, I suppose, unless the neighbours were around. Then he'd just sit there sulking, unsociable to the utmost. Spoiling our lovely evening. It's only because they know he exist that I let him stay amongst us all when we meet. Well, it wouldn't look right having the neighbours around with one member of the family missing. So I suppose I just have to put up with him.

'He's never around now anyway; always in his room. He used to have friends over. Such lovely pleasant boys. I always wondered what they were doing hanging around with him. It just didn't seem fit. Now he's all alone in his room. Only God knows what he does up there for all that time.

'I'll hear him rummaging around up there in his room, eagerly searching for something. Then another minute I'll hear a crashing thud coming from his floor. I don't know what he's throwing to make that sound. Constantly, nearly almost everyday I hear it.

'I don't know what it could be, having stopped going into his room since he was five. His father attended to him from then. I attended to Eleanor. He knows to tidy his room when it's messy. I'm no servant to him. He knows to wash and iron his clothes when dirty. The only thing he doesn't have to do is cook. He's eighteen soon, so now would be a great time to learn - his father could teach him, he's a great cook. As soon as he's eighteen I wash my hands off him. He'll no longer be my responsibility. He'll have to take care of himself.'

Suzie on her neighbours:

EVERYONE'S PERSPECTIVE

'From the moment I came to this neighbourhood I knew I wouldn't fit in unless I was willing to conform. What else was I supposed to do? The way the people first looked at me. Judging me. Sneering at me. I knew. I just knew I had to fit in.

'I was eighteen years old with long bland brunette hair, average skin, tired eyes. They were twenty something looking women. Well kept sleek, lustrous hair. Colour to their faces. Well designed clothes. I was like the black and white version of Pleasantville, and they were the newly coloured scenes of what Reese Witherspoon's character made them. I had to do something. And I had to do it quick!

'Each day I stepped out to go to university or to work, coming back haggard and dishevelled. They'd seem glossier and a lot more vibrant, looking down on me as though I was part of their trash. I didn't even think that any of them worked. They never gave much of an indication as to what they did. Just glossy haired bimbo's with no spark or drive. But nevertheless, I still had to fit in.

'I used to smile pleasantly whenever I'd seen them, but that made them scorn me more; my waves went unnoticed; my hellos were shunned; my smiles were received with poisonous leers. There was just no pleasing those people! My husband was always on Campus. I always got home late. I was lonely and soon angry.

'When I brought home my two children soon after they were born, my husband took some time off studying and he was home a lot more. When he went out he had no problems with the neighbours. I suppose they can tell their own kind. I looked too poor to be living in that neighbourhood, but my husband fitted in perfectly. We made some new friends. Started talking to the neighbours. Suddenly this place wasn't so bad after all. And that's when things changed.

'Some of the women, who were less than polite before, started knocking on our door. My husband and their husbands made friends easily. They'd come over to see the babies and soon we'd get chatting. All of them were rich of course, and I was right; none of them worked.

EVERYONE'S PERSPECTIVE

Their husbands would do all the toiling and brought them home the cash. They could spend as much as they liked. Look as good as they liked. And they didn't have to lift a finger. Just stay at home, look after the children and make sure the house was presentable.

'They soon persuaded me to do the same. None of their husbands were that involved with the house and children. Not like my husband. They said that now that I was a part of their party I should start living like them. So I persuaded my husband - when the children were old enough - to spend more time at work. I could easily manage at home; I had the neighbours. He bought into it and that was that. I was a part of the party.

'My husband finished university with a first in his degree, so it was easy for him to get straight into the job he wanted. Thanks to his father: he got a job at a highly rated company just mere months from finishing his studies. Making a huge salary and having a respectable business tycoon as a father: the girls assured me that we could afford better things. And that it was a husband's duty to provide for his wife. It was only fair seen as I had to give up my dreams to take care of his house and children.

'Having the girls have been a vast improvement. Having people to talk to. People to meet. Makes life just a little more bearable. And we all have so much in common. Of course, they all love their children profoundly. Very much proud of them. Always eager to show them off. I happily oblige with Eleanor; have been showing her off for years. They've watched her grow into a beautiful woman. They see her how I see her. But they also see her brother! They've known the twins since they were babies, so I can't say I don't have a son. I just have to grin and bear their doting on him. Pretend I feel the same.'

Charles Eliot:
Thirty-seven year old Charles Eliot - known as 'Charlie' to his wife, and 'dad' to his children, was an I.T consultant living in Surrey.

He was born to rich parents: his father, a business tycoon renown to a majority of people in the business field, and having had most of them as

EVERYONE'S PERSPECTIVE

apprentices before they started off themselves. And his mother, who started of as his father's secretary before later becoming his business partner.

He was an only child raised by a handful of nannies and was used to a near solitary existence as his parents were always busy with their businesses. From an early age he was taught to be great, and nothing but the best would do. His father was firm in his beliefs of the strong going far, and the weak to be trampled on. He held no prisoners. And he expected the same from his son.

His son was to go far, do great things, and follow in his footsteps. His son was to marry well, produce good children, and live a wealthy sustainable life. He was NOT, however, to pick up a non-middle-class girl! He was NOT to marry a non-middle-class girl. And definitely NOT to have children with a non-middle-class poor girl. Which was exactly what Charles Eliot did.

Charles's father, with fury and disdainful contempt, begrudgingly got his son a job at one of the best known company (thanks to his pleading wife), and quickly washed his hands off him, exclaiming - to his wife's dismay - that they had no son upon this earth. Charles, regretfully, went his separate way.

Charles loved his wife and loved his children dearly. They were the 'apple of his eyes', 'the light of his life' and all other romantic clichés known throughout mankind. His wife and children were truly his life, and no other man was going to stand between them. So Charles left his mother. Left his father and his rules behind, and chose his wife's side, knowing he would never be in company with his parents again. All existence with them was lost.

Charles on his wife:

'My wife and I both met at college. We were studying different things: me, what my father expected of me, and her, Design and Technology.

EVERYONE'S PERSPECTIVE

She wanted to be an interior designer. I really admired that of her. She had no-one behind her, pushing her to be someone as I did, she just knew that that was what she wanted and was working really hard to achieve it.

'Of course I knew she wasn't middle-class and that she had not a lot of money. And I knew that my father would not approve of such a relationship and would almost definitely put an end to it. So I never told him. But mum had sussed it out. She promised to be quiet.

'Suzie was different from the rich girls whom my father approved of; she was quieter and more pleasant. Easy to approach and affable. The other girls wanted to be seen. They were rich with no limits and were cruel with it. They didn't have to struggle, as they already had everything, so ambition wasn't known to them. If they didn't make it into what they claimed they wanted, they could become a part of their parents' business or marry into money and status, never actually having to work for anything. Suzie had ambition and her own free will and drive. And that's what attracted me to her.

'I could be better with her. Never had to pretend to be only interested in power and money. We could talk about other things and relax and have fun. I simply just loved being with her. Sneaking her into my parents' house when they weren't around. Meeting in secret just mere yards from the house. Dad never knew a thing! Then one night, we just lost all track of time and dad came back and caught us in the house.

'We weren't doing anything. Suzie had taken the remote control and I was chasing her. Dad walked in and saw us kissing and that was it really. Dad had heard about her; mum had let her mouth slip. I was basically asked from that moment to choose her or him. I was kicked out pretty much from that moment and that's when Suzie and I started living together before finally getting married and having Eleanor and Simon.

'I saw an instant change in my wife after we had the twins. I don't know what it was but, it had something to do with Simon. She wasn't like other mother's who I'd seen with their children; she seemed remote, even indifferent, until all of a sudden I was left taking sole care or Simon,

EVERYONE'S PERSPECTIVE

and when I asked her what was wrong, she didn't reply. I had considered post-natal-depression at first, but Suzie assured me that she was fine, just a little bit tired. It was nothing to worry about. I didn't entirely believe her. But I just watched things from then.'

Charles on his son:

'From the moment Simon was born I loved him, obviously. I love both my children. Simon, though, is the image of his mother; same black hair, same lips, the same eyes. He definitely looks like Suzie.

'From the age of five, Simon has always spent most of the time a child usually spends with their mother, with me, so Simon and I have grown pretty close. We've done the father-son thing: playing kick about in the back garden, teaching him to ride a bike (though I did also teach his sister) and watching sports on the T.V.

'Simon is a good kid. Never been in trouble with anyone or with anything. I've watched him grow from the innocent young child with so much curiosity, to the man that he almost is today. He's nothing like how I was when I was younger. Twenty years ago, at his age, I'd have been running around with my friends, venturing new things, not to mention spending copious amount of time with his mother. Simon doesn't do any of that. His friends have all stopped coming around, and he's stopped going to them. I've never seen him with any girls, and he's always stuck in his room. That room must have something really good for it to possess his time for so long. I almost think that if it wasn't for going to school, he'd probably never leave that room. But all the same: he spends far too much time in there. It isn't normal.'

Charles on his daughter:

'The most sweetest and profoundly sensible girl. Never was a trouble in all of her seventeen years. She differs considerably from her brother and

EVERYONE'S PERSPECTIVE

I've always thought that her mother held a special soft spot for her. Though, it is me who she looks like.

'Eleanor has always been the perfect child; she never purposely did anything wrong; never cheated in an exam, and has always been polite and affable. Obviously, I haven't been around that much to watch the children grow, but Eleanor has certainly turned out well.

'She's smart and caring, and well disciplined. Never been in trouble in school. And has always known where she's wanted to go. I'm so proud of her and I know that her grand-mother would be too.

'Eleanor and Simon have never seen their grand-parents, but not from a lack of trying. Suzie has always asked - practically pleaded with me to let the children see their grand-parents. Of course, she's never known that my father disowned us; my father cleverly waited upon Suzie's departure from the house before giving me the ultimatum: him or her. She doesn't know that I chose her and that with that: in disowning me, my father also disowned her and our children.

'She always wants to know why my parents never ring or come round to visit. Or why, alternatively, don't we go to them. The excuses are getting tiring. Eleanor would like to see her grand-mother. She has asked about her a few times but somehow the timing's never been right to explain to her. To explain to them. So I just dig up another excuse until they all seem satisfied, and wait for the next time that the questions come pouring in.'

Charles on his work:

'From when I was old enough my father started teaching me about his business. Teaching me about colleagues, about his riches and what it could do. I was expected to shut up and listen, pay close attention and never question my father's mind. My own mind, on the other hand, I questioned frequently.

'My father wanted me to follow in his footsteps. Walk the same paths

EVERYONE'S PERSPECTIVE

as he had done. Attend the same schools. Attend the same college. Walk into his profession. And I was doing it. No questions asked.

'I went to the same pre-school and high school as he did. I went to the same college as he had done. Had some of the same teachers. Was taught the same lessons. But I couldn't be like him. I was not my father, but my father never saw it.

'I wanted to be able to make my own decisions. Make my own mistakes and change courses. But it was not my father's way. I often think about what I could have been, given the chance. Maybe I might have naturally chosen business and I.T, but not under his guardianship, and not under his rules. Or maybe I might have been a lawyer, or even a chef! Who knows what I could have done.

'My father's not the sort of person that listens, you listen to him. He can't and won't have it any other way. He's been set in his ways from when he was young and has never steered from it. He likes control. He likes money. And most importantly, he likes power. Without it he would be nothing: debased and lower than what he could tolerate. Pitiful, pathetic and down right worthless. And that is why my dad looks down on the poor; because to be like them would mean that he had not succeeded, and that to him is weak. A position that would leave him powerless. Vulnerable to all those around him.

'My father's so good, he married his secretary and made it look like a good investment. She'll always be lower than him though it is her charm and looks that seals his deals. Plus, having a wife and child makes him seem a bit more approachable.

'My father married for wealth, not for love. Wife and kids means better prospects. Better connections. I married for love. My children were conceived in love. I wish I could say the same about me. I was also an investment. When I left my father's home and joined my wife, I had it clear into my head that I would never make the same mistakes as my father. I would never push my kids to be something that they weren't. Do something they didn't want to do. And I regret nothing.

EVERYONE'S PERSPECTIVE

'After leaving university, my money cut off and no means of getting a job straight away, my dad did me his one last and bitter favour of getting me a job at one of his business acquaintance's company. He made sure I started of low; low wages, dysfunctional hours, weekends away from my family. I begged on my life to have some time off after my wife had the twins. They weren't best pleased. So when my wife asked me to do extra hours at work, it was the least I could do for the company, as the old animosity for my time off was still present.

'I've fallen into the job now. Very used to it. Very used to the colleagues: some old, some new. We even spend some hours after work just killing time. Talking about our families whilst having some light beverages. Going over some of our work plans. Talking about holidays.

'I'm not too fond of my job; been doing it too long. It's become stagnant, dull, repetitive. I would have left by now if it wasn't for Suzie. She likes things just the way they are. She likes our extra income. Our special privileges. Her new society of friends. None of that actually matters to me. I'd rather be doing something I liked.'

Eleanor Eliot:

Eleanor sat in her room crying. She was going over and over and over again into her mind everything that had happened. Everything that had taken place. Everything she had missed. Everything she had just started to see. To hear. To feel. Everything was so messed up, and she didn't know what to do.

How was she to handle the situated by herself? How was she supposed to terminate it without anyone else finding out? She couldn't tell her mother; she'd be too disappointed. And she definitely couldn't tell her father; he would be besides himself in mental anguish! He'd probably think it was all her fault. That she should have been more vigilant. Like the second party was totally innocent! Like they weren't also in the wrong! She didn't know what to do. What would they do when they

EVERYONE'S PERSPECTIVE

found out about it? It couldn't be kept a secret forever. It was already becoming highly conspicuous. She had to do something before it was too late and she was suspecting that her mother had noticed.

Her face was sopping in tears. Eyes red and agitated, she still couldn't bring herself to stop. Her dark brown eyes looked down at her bedding as she sobbed into her pillow. Her brunette hair fell over her face washing itself onto her sopping cheeks. She gripped her duvet in all her anguish, struggling to breathe, struggling to think.

Eleanor on her brother:

'My brother is falling apart. He thinks that no-one has noticed, but I have! I am his sister. I know. There is nothing he can do and hide from me without me finding out sooner or later. I only hoped I'd have found this out from before. I only hope I'm not too late. That it's not too late for him. I have to save him.

'I've seen him. Leaving the dinner table early without eating anything. Wasting away into his room, collapsing on the floor, hallucinating. "Blacked out" for hours and never knowing where he is. Coming in late looking haggard and wan. Over sleeping in the morning when he should have been up for school. He's completely deteriorating and I don't even think he cares. I don't even know if he's noticed.

'A year ago my brother looked fine; his hair had body; HE had a body. He looked like he had blood in his veins and his eyes weren't blank and distant. Now he looks a total wreck; disorientated, disparate. He used to have friends, hang out and have fun. Now that's all changed. I'm not the only one who's noticed: his friends have noticed too.

'Gary, Peter and Paul, they've all seen the difference in him. They know something is up. They don't hang out with him anymore because of his newly developed tendencies. They think he's strange. They've each told me that with their own mouths. They stopped answering his phone calls because his speech was always slurred and he wasn't talking anything

EVERYONE'S PERSPECTIVE

intelligible. And they stopped calling round the house because they were fed up of having to support his stance, and covering for him. They said they couldn't bear to be around him anymore. He looked too remote.

'We all hang out now in the school yard. I wouldn't say that we were 'friends' friends, more like acquaintances. We sit down and talk mostly, mainly about Simon. That's the thing all of us have in common: Simon. I haven't told them that he's doing drugs - what else could it be? I just act on the fact that he's changed and they all agree. I don't know how I'm going to help Simon, but to do that I'm going to need their help.

'We've been planning on how best to get to Simon. We know we need to get him isolated (though he already is) to be able to help him. It's kind of like cornering him. Making him face up to his problems with nowhere to hide. He needs to be completely alone; no people around him; no chance of there being anyone to interrupt. So we can't do it in school - though there have been plenty of opportunities, and we can't do it at home with mother around. But we don't know about that one yet. So we have no choice but to look at him when he walks past. Explore all of our options.

'We know that he's noticed us all huddled up together, and that makes it all the more harder. It's proving difficult to get to him as he now seems a bit more aware of us, even suspicious. Simon's a clever boy, and I don't think the drugs have destroyed his brains so much that he's completely deluded by us. My time is running out though; I won't be here forever, and I need to get to him before it's too late. So, therefore, I know I'm going to have to tell the boys about his drug habit soon.'

Eleanor on her mother:

'When I was younger I used to adore my mother. I might not have followed her around as much as Simon but I generally loved being around my mother. She was so caring and attentive, and so consoling towards me, I thought she was the best mother in the world. As I grew older,

EVERYONE'S PERSPECTIVE

however, I started to see the change.

'My mother was only ever nice to me. She was never that nice to Simon. She used to pick me up and cuddle me, kiss me goodnight, say "good morning" when I woke up with so much zeal. But Simon, she used to ignore. The woman was unbelievably cold towards him, and he was only a child then. An innocent. She ignored him when he cried, would evade him when he hurt himself, would walk out the room when she saw him. It was a wonder that she still fed him, the amount of venom she unwittingly showed towards him. She thought that no-one was watching. But I saw it all.

'She doesn't like me being around my brother. She never has. The more time we spend apart the happier she seems. But she can't always have things her own way. And it's about time she learnt that.

'Dad seems completely oblivious towards her misdeeds. He worships the ground she walks on and she knows it. She can get him to do anything and she's very proud of that. Like working harder at the office so that she can spend his money and fit in with the neighbours. She always advises me to concentrate on my studies and make something of myself as she once wanted to. But if she wanted to be a designer so badly, why did she give up uni? The amount of money she has spent from dad's job would have been more than enough for her to continue her studies after we were old enough and do the career she always goes on about.

'It's not my place to slag off my mother. Dad needs to find out about her himself, I'm just not quite sure he can see that far inside of her. She thinks I don't know that she's been in my room, rooting up all my things, going through my files. She's been doing it for a while now, right about the same time I starting checking up on Simon. The nerve of that woman going through my things! If I had anything to hide I wouldn't hide it in my room; that's far too obvious. Oh no! Whatever I'm hiding is with Paul: he takes care of them all until it's time. Besides, I've been watching her go through my room. From the very first time she started rooting it up I've been watching it on Paul's computer. My web cam is always on.

EVERYONE'S PERSPECTIVE

'I think it's clear to me that my mother doesn't like Simon, and Simon doesn't like her. Dad's the only person left into this family who still dotes on her. Even grand-dad (I'm not sure about grand-ma), doesn't like her, but it's easy to see how it can happen.

'The sooner I finish school the better. Only a few more months left till our exams then life will change, hopefully for the better. And I will be on my way to better things. I only wish I could take Simon with me. My only hope is to get him on the right path in time. Because when I leave school it won't be the only thing I'll be leaving.'

Eleanor on her father:

'I've always liked dad best; he's so very kind and sweet - too sweet perhaps when it comes to mum, but he's always been nice to the both of us. I'm glad I look more like my dad than my mum, that would seriously offend me. Poor Simon. He hates my mother but he actually looks like her. A constant reminder of the one that hates you.

'Dad's always working. He misses out on a lot. From when I can remember my dad's always been sort of absent. It was just rare glimpses of him running through the door to get to work and then coming in late from work. Everything he does seems to be about work. It's a shame.

'If mum was the one who went to work we'll probably have a happier life. Dad's really attentive. It can be seen by the amount of effort he puts in his work, but it's also built into him, naturally.

'If there is one thing I'd like it'd be for dad to see the truth. For dad to see the real relationship between mum and Simon. How mother shuns away from him. The hurt and anger in Simon's eyes. I want my dad to see what sort of a woman he married. I want him to see her the way that I have seen her for all this time behind the mask. Behind the fake smiles to the neighbours, and to him, and everyone. So there's only one thing I can do. The truth must come out. I don't know what he'll be like or how he'll act, but it needs to be done.'

EVERYONE'S PERSPECTIVE

Eleanor on herself:

'I have a lot of friends in and around school and I like spending time with them all. There are simply too many to put names to but, I value them all the same. My friends and I would normally hook up in school in and out of lessons and spend our time just chatting and lazing about, and when school is over I'd normally go back to one of their homes - I never take them in my house though they have been outside of it. They don't mind though; there's more freedom at their homes, and it's too embarrassing what with Simon's problem and all.

'I have a lot more girlfriends than I do boyfriends. I would say a strong ten girls to about four boys and we all hang out together the majority of the time, though we do split sometimes into smaller groups or just by ourselves.

'I love my friends. If I didn't have them I don't know how I would past the time. Being stuck in the house all the time isn't my idea of fun. Hanging at my friends' homes and clubbing is so much better, though mum doesn't know I go clubbing. But, that's not the only thing she doesn't know.

'I met Paul one night when I was clubbing with a group of friends. He's not a part of our crowd so we never see each other, I only ever saw him with Simon , Gary and his brother when they all used to be friends. Although Paul, Gary and his brother: Peter, are all still pretty tight. I was quite surprised to see him and we got talking.

'He told me how him and the others were noticing certain changes in Simon, at the time, I hadn't noticed anything. It was because of this that got me observing Simon more than usual. I started splitting my time between my friends and Paul and his lot, and that's how our planning came about. But as time drew on Paul and I started spending a lot more time together. I really enjoyed his company.

'Me and Paul, unlike the other two, got along really well. I started

EVERYONE'S PERSPECTIVE

spending time at his house outside of our "Simon plotting", and we would just talk and mess about. We grew really close and now we are together. My mother wouldn't like the idea of me having a boyfriend; she's warned me enough times. But this is not her life. And I'm not stupid like her. I know what I'm doing.

'Paul and I have been together for a few months now and we're pretty serious about each other. We both plan to go to the same uni, though, we will be in different departments, studying different subjects. And also both plan to live in the same place. Mother thinks I'm going to stay in Surrey whilst I study but my plans are very different. I can't stand the idea of being in the same house as her any longer, so I've just been praying for school to hurry up and finish.

'After our end of year exams and graduation, Paul and I are moving to Oxford. We've already applied for our chosen universities (more than one each), but they are all within reach of Oxford so we won't be that far from each other if anything stops us both going to Oxford. Although, I think there's a strong possibility that we'll both get in Oxford from our individual careers advise sessions. The professor from Oxford seemed really pleased with me, and Paul said the same about his session. I'm really excited.

'Paul and I have accumulated our money, and we each have enough for our tickets - which Paul is going to buy, and enough money to share a flat for at least a year. We both have trust funds set up for our studies so tuition fees are not a problem. We just need to gather up our things nearing the end of school, after our exams, then we can leave this place.

'I know it's a lot to ask for: for Simon to acknowledge his problems before we leave, but I don't have that much time left. If only I'd had known about this from earlier, things might have been a lot more clearer, and I would have had a lot more time to sort him out. I'm not asking for him to be clean by the time that we leave; it takes more time than that I'm sure. I just want him to have a clear view in front of him, he has no choice but to stay here and still under our parents' roof. I won't be there

EVERYONE'S PERSPECTIVE

to look after him anymore. He needs to look after himself.'

The neighbours and Mr Galloway.
The neighbours:

Four very stylishly elegant women sat around a coffee table oozing off richness and poised dignity in an extremely pristine living area. All of them talking generously about a neighbourhood family.

'Of course, I never saw the big attraction myself. She always seemed so plain and uncultivated compared to the rest of us. Never would have given her the light of day if you ask me.' came the rich sonorous voice of one. 'Always so readily willing to please. Always wanted to fit in.' She finished, and took a sip of coffee.

'Oh, I remember her pitiful attempt to get our attention: waving that oddly thin hand of hers, lavishing us with smiles. Her voice was so weak and strained. Never understood why she never just walked on. If we never said hello first we were never going to be interested.'

'Yes, but, some people just never learn. Do they?'

The four of them laughed mirthlessly. All spite and scorn writ over their faces. No compassion or humility was seen.

'The only reason we allow her space is because of her husband.'

'Oh yes! He could do so much better.'

'Never saw the attraction myself.' Repeated the first. All of them nodded in agreement.

'You could just tell. Couldn't you? Couldn't you just tell?'

All of them nodded again. It seemed clear between them who and what the conversation was about. And what the general feeling was towards it and them.

'I never saw a person so odiously poor! No fashion sense! No style!-'

'And not to mention: no self-respect-'

'Or self-esteem.'

'Completely offensive. Almost humiliating if you ask me.' Continued

EVERYONE'S PERSPECTIVE

the first.

She took another sip of coffee with such pleasing grace that it was clear to see how a person like her - like any of them - could be truly offended by a person less of what she was. Her glossy black hair kept neatly pinned up in one with two sleek ringlets dropping down on either side of her face. Her make-up was immaculate - as the rest of them, perfectly matching the shade of her attire as she sat with perfect stance projecting her complacent magnificence.

'It is through sheer pity that she is allowed with us. Would you believe that my husband told me of her husband being someone he went to school with? I could not believe it! Him of our class. His father so powerful and he marries a girl like that! Utterly shameful. Yet! It is not him who offends us. She does all by herself.

'Marrying him for his money I suspect. She never seems to do anything. No charities. No funds. Although, she would not fit in with the crowd.' She laughed a deep and cold laugh. The others followed suit.

'But, as I was saying, my husband and hers went to the same school. Never really mixed in the same circle, but anyone of that school is of real high rank. We accept him fully.'

She sipped her last sip of coffee before placing it down in it's saucer and turned to the woman sitting next to her. Her hair was blond and remarkably straight, and quite long, resting on her back. Her features strong and rectangular. High cheekbones and sharp penetrating grey eyes. She spoke with an acute French accent.

'My husband and I have made our own money. Him with his firm and me through my family. Never would my father have allowed me to depend solely on a man. He had me working in the bank from when I can assume I was a baby, it is what I know. I have made my fortune with a range of Swiss banks.'

'Of course.' Accented the women in near unison.

'He would cry shame of me if I laid dependent,' she continued. 'Not to mention with children around. What kind of an example is that to

EVERYONE'S PERSPECTIVE

set?'

'We lead by example.' Said another, as the women once again accented.

'Such precious children though.'

'Ah yes. Simply lovely.'

'Though the boy seems a bit depressed.'

'Yes.' They all agreed again.

'But who wouldn't be with a mother like that.' Exclaimed the third woman.

Her face bore a disgusted countenance. Her black eyes tightly compressed, scrutinizing the others.

'She always seems so distant from him. No love is present there.'

'No love whatsoever.'

'Such a shame.' She said shaking her head.

'And you know,' said the first, 'if she would only acknowledge him he might be a bit more pleasant. Less sulky I think.'

'I agree.' Said the third.

Mr Galloway:

'Simon used to be a good student, fairly detached sometimes, but overall a good student. Recently however, it has been brought to my attention just how detached he has become; his work has slackened and his concentration is non-existent. He merely sits in the classroom and stares into space, and that's assuming that he's there at all.

'He worries me does Simon. The once bright, intelligent student now walks into the classroom with circles and bags under his eyes and always looks tired. I am not the only one who has noticed. The other teachers have started to voice their concern, and some of the pupils whisper about his appearance and odd behaviour when they think I'm not listening. I tell them all to be quiet and get on with their work, but I have to admit, I feel the same.

EVERYONE'S PERSPECTIVE

'Never once in my life have I seen a student deteriorate so rapidly. And never have I seen one decide over night that they no longer care. I would say it was neglect at home but Eleanor seems to be a thriving student and never has put a foot wrong. So it leaves a big question mark over the concern of Simon.

'His parents seem such lovely folks; eager and understanding. His mother is always so cheerful and pleasant, and his father - what I've seen of him, seems very much the same. Simon comes from a good home and a good family; they don't seem to be in want of anything so I just can't seem to put my finger on what might be the cause of all this.'

Mr Galloway had lived in Surrey all his life and had been a teacher for nearly half that time. During his career as a History teacher it is needless to say that he had come across a majority of pupils: good, bad and all that's in-between. But in his profession, though some students had started off low and made their steady and vast improvements, none of them had been so near the top and sunk so low to the bottom in such a short time. Most children who started to show and shine at educational weaknesses usually had profound reasons and excuses for their work to steadily turn to it's worse.

Some of them had family matters too great for them to comprehend: the stress of moving home, moving to a new school and bereavement would usually be the most common. Having to split their time between divorced parents was a close second. The majority of the children who attended Lake Hill Grammar came from an affluent and well educated background, only a small minority not-so-wealthy children who were extremely gifted attended the school and they seemed to be the ones who made the most progress. Simon, according to Mr Galloway, didn't really have a reason to be going off the rails, but somehow, he continued to fall more and more over the edge, and with the last few fingers that he had holding on to the border before his (possibly inevitable) tremendous fall, he seemed to be willing his fingers to let go and send him to his doom.

'I've had very brief encounters with Mr Eliot, Simon and Eleanor's father. But, he is a very pleasant chap and always ready to hear the progress of his children's education. He seems an avid listener and one can see he is very interested. Whenever we have a parents viewing day for them to see their children's report, if Mr Eliot is available he'll make himself present. And he has such a charming wife. One cannot see a better couple about.'

Eleanor Eliot:

'Finally school is at a close. I just had my exams near a month ago and soon I'll get my results. I can't wait; after that Paul and I can leave, they'll be nothing else holding us back. Well, apart from Simon of course. Before I leave I have to clear the air, but until then, I'm just waiting.'

Simon Eliot:

'Exams have been in session but, unlike everyone else I didn't take mine, so, unlike everyone else, I already know my results. Just to think, just a year before now I would have done anything to get good grades, but now I can't even make my brain work properly. But that is my fault.

'I've up my drugs, not the intake, just the drugs. I now have amphetamines but it's not how I expected it to be, I just can't function. But now, I definitely can't stop. I need help quick before I sink further. But at the same time, I kind of don't want help. Maybe things are better this way. Mother won't notice me no matter what I do, and father's still so busy he expects everything to stay as they are: for us to grow but not to ever change. If he can't see the superficiality in mother now he never will.'

Simon on his sister:

EVERYONE'S PERSPECTIVE

'There is something up with Elle; from what I have noticed she's never in the house anymore, I mean, I might be out of it a lot of the time but when I do come around she's never there. It feels so empty without Elle. When she's not around I feel kind of lost. I can't explain it but I do.

'I've never been in her room uninvited but I can tell she's not there; there's no sound from her computer, I can't hear her footsteps, there's just nothing. Though I do sometimes hear slight rummaging coming from her room. I don't understand, 'cause if it isn't Elle, then I don't know where or who it's coming from.

'I spend a lot of time in my room now a days, for obvious reasons. I figure, if everyone sees me as invisible then I might as well not be seen. They don't ask for me. Mother never really calls me for or about anything. Sometimes not even for dinner, though sometimes I do catch a glimpse of her walking from outside my room. Mother ignoring me is to be expected now, but I never thought that Elle would start to do the same.

'I see them, though: her and Paul when I'm looking out of the window, they're always together now, even at school. Before there was Paul, Elle and the others, now it's just Paul and Elle all the time. Together. She doesn't even spend time with her old friends anymore; I hear their voices travelling through the floorboards asking for her: how they haven't seen her in a while, how she hasn't been returning any of their calls, or E-mails. "What is wrong with her?", "Do you (mother) know where she is?" It makes me sick!

'I have no-one, not even Elle anymore. All my friends have gone to her and she ignores the others. And spending time with Paul! What is that about? Sometimes I get so angry. I get so frustrated I just want to smash something. Anything so long as it breaks. Just a release. I knew she would leave me.

'She spends just as much time in her room as I do when she's not with Paul. I wonder what she's up to? Spending so much time locked up in there. Quietly. Silently to herself. Well forget her anyway! What's the

EVERYONE'S PERSPECTIVE

point? If she doesn't need me, then, I don't need her! I'm better off alone anyway.'

Eleanor Eliot:

'Well ... I have my results back now. I did pretty well, and now there's definitely nothing holding me back (apart from the obvious). No more school or sixth-form. I am totally free now. Paul and I have been looking forward to this day and we have been doing everything possible to meet it. So here it is:

'Over the past month I've been moving my things bit by bit to Paul's room. It's pretty safe there as no-one goes in without his permission. He's the lucky one! Well, bit by bit, mainly at night, I've been moving things to Paul's place; he picks me up just a few yards from the house so we can transport my things. No-one in my house is the wiser, so I've been getting away with it so far, not that they can stop me now anyway. I've been very careful to only take small things to not draw attention to myself, and I've been shifting and moving things around in my wardrobe and draws, so no-one notices that anything's missing. Paul has a lot of space in his room: a lot of storage space, so no-one's going to notice even if they should go into his room.

'My room is almost empty now. It's getting harder to conceal the emptiness, but I don't think I care that much. The only person that would possibly see the difference would be mum, and she shouldn't be in my room anyway! If she does ask, however, I'll just make something up - about friends or a trip or something, other than that I'll try to avoid her at all cost. I really don't have the patience for her anyhow.

'We're thinking about leaving in the next two weeks. We're going to take the train to Oxford and maybe stay in a B&B until we can sort out a flat. We'll have some weeks before starting uni and Paul already has a job sorted there thanks to his uncle, so we'll be alright for money, so that just leaves me to get a part-time job. I have a few places listed and they

EVERYONE'S PERSPECTIVE

do good pays for students so that shouldn't be a problem. I'm just waiting to get going really.'

Eleanor on her mother:

'Mum's been playing the right little hostess recently. She's been keeping little dinner parties almost on a daily basis for the neighbours. It's funny because I've seen them each going to each others homes, uninvited to my mother of course. It's just a bit strange.

'Nearly everyday she's been throwing these sickly sweet feigned civil dinner parties. Getting dressed up in these obviously not so cheap dresses to try and fit in with the other women - I wonder what dad would say about her spending habit if he knew? And she's been trying relentlessly to get me to join in. It's almost as though she knows something. Every time I get in proximity of her she starts acting really nice asking me all these questions: "Where are you going?", "What are you doing?", "Do you want to join me for dinner?", "Do I feel like doing anything (with her) today?" She is up to something. Trying to stop me from going out, almost locking me in the house. I asked her why she didn't ask Simon to join her instead of me. That seemed to shut her up for a bit. She left me alone for a few days, but it was still only short lived.

'The neighbours have been very courteous to me though. They always say "Hello" and ask how I'm doing and how I'm getting along in school. They seem really genuine with me at least. Mother just doesn't seem to get it though. She can't keep me here. I'm not a little girl anymore. She has no power over me and I'll be damned if she does. No amount of feigned sweetness is going to change anything. It's too late now.'

Eleanor on Paul and Friends:

'It hasn't all been about Paul and mine's departure from here. Simon has always been our main concern and though the four of us haven't managed

EVERYONE'S PERSPECTIVE

to help Simon out of the hole he's put himself into as planned, we have finally been getting somewhere.

'Paul was the only one who I told of Simon's suspected drug use - about the "black outs", hallucinations and others. He said that it sounded like Simon has been having bad "trips" and he has become too tolerant to stop taking the drugs. I didn't like the sound of that because Simon never seems to be in the best of moods and the drugs have been steadily making them worse; the more he takes, the worse he becomes. Paul said it sounded like "LSDs" and although they might not be addictive they do have a way of making the person become rapidly tolerant, which sounds exactly like Simon, according to his research.

'We had been working on it one on one at the beginning, that's also one of the reasons I started spending more time at his place, we also made sure that his brother was out before we met up so that we could have more time to test the theory. We didn't want to mention anything to the others yet until we were sure we were absolutely right. Though we all still met up on school grounds to discuss the matter at hand.

'Paul and I decided to catch Simon at it if possible, so I set up a web cam in my room just in case he should ever feel the need to go in my room, and I always made it pretty obvious to the whole house when I was going out so as to entice him to go in my room, but he never did. Instead I caught my mother there searching through my stuff. I was shocked, but she'll never find anything; all of our research and plans are kept in Paul's room. So we had to find another way.

'From then on I decided to stay close to Simon. To sort of follow his lead. I began to scrutinize his every move, to walk in his every step. I wanted to catch him with the drugs without his knowing. I started to follow him to his room and sort of linger near it's threshold. I'd pretend to go into my room when actually waiting for him to begin his habit. It never took long; within minutes of entering his room he's go into the corner of his cupboard, retrieve his silver watchcase and take out a bag containing the drugs, and, as Paul guessed, it was LSD. Through the slit

EVERYONE'S PERSPECTIVE

of door I saw all this and I thought I would have been prepared; I went over it enough times in my head, but I wasn't.

'To see Simon take the drugs and watch him as it took effect was unnerving. To see him on the floor experiencing his so very common "trips" made me sick, but I know for definite now and I also needed the proof. I went into his room once and removed some of the drugs, but he looked so helpless as I walked past him that I stooped down and stroked his hair. I don't know if he could hear me but I told him it'd be alright then I left. I would stand there sometimes at the edge of his door just watching him. I don't think he knew I was there.

'Once I obtained the proof and showed it to Paul there could be no denying what he was taking and so we told the others. We decided to book him into a clinic and get him some counselling but they were all so expensive, we couldn't do it by ourselves. I've asked dad some time before about my grandparents. He's always been very evasive of the discussion, but I've gathered that grandma is the most hospitable of the two. Dad wouldn't tell me where they lived and how to get in contact with them; always going around the subject, so I decided to take matters into my own hands.

'If mum can snoop in my room, then I can snoop in hers. I went through their drawers to try and find something. Anything, to lead me closer to my grandparents, and dad, carelessly enough, had a card with his father's work contacts. And in his address book I found both their work and home numbers, and an address that was crossed out. I copied it out and have been trying to get through to grandma ever since.

'Every time I tried the home number: a male voice answered - I'm assuming that's grand-dad, so I always hung up. But I kept trying until finally a woman answered. She sounded really nice; pleasant, welcoming. I don't know if you can tell all that from: "Hello? Is there anyone there?" but I felt it. My grandmother!

'I was so shocked and scared and happy, I nearly put the phone down, but I kept my nerve and said: "Grandma ... Is that you?" She gasped and I

EVERYONE'S PERSPECTIVE

instantly felt scared; I thought she might put the phone down or tell me never to call again or say I had the wrong number, but she just said "Oh my God!" breathlessly. I explained who I was but she said she already knew as dad and her had never lost touch and he'd spoken about us (Simon and I) relentlessly. She said she was sorry she had never come round but due to circumstances, it was better that way.

'After our emotional catch up I started to tell her all on Simon and how he needed help and how we couldn't help him, and how all was at a loss if we couldn't. I think I might have been getting a bit hysterical because before long she was telling me to calm down and breathe. I did as she said and she said she could help with the cost and how she knew of a good clinic with good counsellors who helped people in Simon's condition. I was so happy I actually started to cry. I couldn't believe it! Grandma and I have been conversing in secret ever since. Only Paul knows about it.'

Suzie on her daughter:

'There is definitely something going on with Eleanor and I don't like it. Her constant leaving of the house worries me as it is not to her friends that she goes to, so it leaves me wondering what she is up to.

'Her friends have been around asking for her, saying how they haven't seen her in a while and how they are all wondering where she is or who she is with. I'm beginning to ask the same questions myself because before then I have always thought that it was them who she was with, but now all that has changed. Eleanor, I can see now, has changed. Whenever I see her nowadays she is always heading for the door without an explanation as to where she is going or who she will be with. It is very disturbing.

'She seems less and less like the daughter I know and love and more like someone I don't know. And it is not just her actions, it is also her manner. Her staying away from her friends is not normal, especially for a

EVERYONE'S PERSPECTIVE

girl as bright and sociable as her. She won't speak to me anymore and the smiles she produces now seems a bit strained, almost forced. I have to get at the bottom of this. All this secrecy is not healthy.

'I'm ashamed to say, once again, that I've taken most profusely to my old habit of searching her room. I had stopped for some time because all seemed well, but now I am convinced she's up to something.

'The first few times of my newly returned search seemed ok; everything seemed to be in order, there was nothing incriminating lying around or otherwise, and I should know because I searched everywhere. Now, on the other hand, I've noticed that certain things are disappearing. Her clothes for one seem to be disappearing by the day; her wardrobe and drawers lay almost bare. I was concerned before but now I don't know what to think.

'I have tried to catch her in the act, to corner her, but nothing seems to work. It is not for my health that I throw so many dinner parties - once a week seems fine to me, but I have to try and delay her some how without her knowing what I'm up to. I just need a little more time to find out what she is doing!

'Thus far, as her clothes, amongst other things, continue to vanish, I have not been able to see how they are vanishing. Eleanor seems clean when she leaves the house; she leaves sometimes freely; without bag; too small a pocket to hold anything; and her clothes are just not big enough for her to stuff things underneath them without me noticing. There is nothing. And I am beginning to fall into panic.

'She wouldn't even show me her exam results when she finally got them. I practically had to plead with her to let me see them. I was beginning to think that she didn't do well - don't know what I would have done - but she did great. I don't know why she didn't want to show me. Or tell me. It is really strange. She doesn't even want to tell me what university she plans to go to. Or what she plans to study. Anyway … she won't be that far off when the time comes for her to start university. She'll still be living right here in the house. That I know.'

EVERYONE'S PERSPECTIVE

Suzie on Simon:

'Oh! Simon. I honestly don't know what I'm going to do with him. The boy is so strange. I always knew I never liked him for a reason; he is such a weirdo; locking himself away like that; keeping himself hidden. He's nothing like his father. But I suppose they do have other things in common.

'Failing his exams! I always knew he would end up with nothing. No matter what Charlie thinks of him he'll never amount to anything. Eleanor got all her results - as I knew she would. She'll be going places unlike that Simon. Oh well. I said I'll be rid of him by eighteen, and it's just what I intend to do.

'It's his and Eleanor's birthday soon - both will be eighteen, both will be adults, and I want Simon out of here. It's only a shame that he failed his exams for the simple reason of him being able to live near a university, but now that is impossible, I'll just have to find another way. Charlie won't want to leave so I'll just have to persuade him some how. It's been far too long that that boy has been taking up space in this house.'

Eleanor on Simon:

'I haven't been in the house much; now that nearly all my things are gone I've been staying at Paul's for safe keeping. Mum keeps trying to trap me whenever I'm there and I've had enough of her stupid dinner parties. I can't stand another one of her pretentious superfluous "parties" any longer, and I'm not the only one. Her "guests" are looking a bit peed off but of course mother hasn't noticed. She's been so busy trying to trap me, she hasn't even seen what's in front of her nose. Of course this makes it difficult for me to check on Simon.

'I thought there was something wrong with him before but now! He's

EVERYONE'S PERSPECTIVE

not showing the same symptoms of what he had before. He's changed. Simon was always nice even with his problem but now he's peed off. From the little bit of time that I've been spending at home I've seen a different side to him.

'I hear him mumbling in his room. Talking to himself. And I know it's to himself because nobody comes to visit him and it wasn't his T.V or radio; he destroyed them. That's another thing that he's been doing. He's been really irritable lately, getting angry over the slightest things and mashing things up.

'He was angry some days ago and slammed the door a few times - I thought he was just letting off some steam but he then started to tear things off his desk and threw his T.V against the wall. Sparks were flying but he didn't seem to care. He could have set the place on fire! He then took his stereo and started smashing it repeatedly against the wall, even though there was hardly anything left. He smashed his mirror, was throwing things on the floor. I've never seen him like that before.

'I went in his room to try and stop him; I was always good at calming him down, but now! He nearly laid into me. He physically threw me against the wall, never letting go of my shoulders the whole time and started shaking me. I've never been so scared. He's always been so nice. I don't understand. He just kept saying "What are you doing with Paul?" Each time he said it he became more and more diffused until he just started screaming at me. I couldn't get out of there faster. I managed to push him off, not being able to console him, and ran out of the house. He is not right. We need to get him some help quickly or I'm afraid he might go mad.

'When I did return home Simon seemed not to have noticed how on edge he had made me; he just looked a bit tense and depressed. Maybe he didn't even notice me. He's been locked up in his room a lot more than usual. He never comes out and he won't speak to anyone - not that there's anyone to speak to, but he never seems to want to speak to me. He looks at me as though I've let him down or something. Like I'm no

EVERYONE'S PERSPECTIVE

longer human. He unnerves me.'

Eleanor on her grandmother:

'I don't speak about Simon to anyone else outside of Paul and those who it concerns. Peter and Gary are taking it upon themselves to stay into the background but they say that they'll visit Simon when he's in the clinic and help out from there as much as they can. Grandma is a real help.

'We've been talking on the phone a lot. I've really grown to love my grandma though we've only ever spoken through the phone. She's been a real help. I don't know what I would have done without her. She's spoken to Paul a few times. She says he sounds like a nice young man and she hopes that everything works out for us. I had to tell her about us moving. It's actually in two days. Everything is sorted out and that's why grandma and I have been speaking so frequently. Two weeks have really flown away fast. Grandma knows of the urgency to get Simon in a clinic quickly before we leave.

'She told me that she has Simon booked in to begin treatment and counselling the day we leave. I am so relieved. The clinic is in London near where grandma and grand-dad live, so it's not that far off. Simon's going to be kept there until he's better or until the money runs out, but grandma's been assuring me that Simon will only leave when he's better, no time sooner.

'Grandma's even agreed to come down to help with the transition. She says she wants to see her two grand-children before we both leave to go our separate ways. I can't wait to see her but I also feel so sad; the first Simon and I will see our grandma is under these circumstances. It all feels so wasted. But we've both promised to stay in touch and she says I'm free to visit her whenever I like, and she'll be a recurrent visitor to Simon. She also exclaimed that she can't wait to see her son. She'll be coming down in two days and will be coming alone. Grand-dad knows nothing of this.'

EVERYONE'S PERSPECTIVE

Eleanor on her grandma:

'Grandma came down as promised. I can't believe it. I'd never seen her before but she looked really great. Really pleasant and courteous, just like how she sounded on the phone, but in the flesh. She said she came down by the train. Left out from six in the morning. Grand-dad had already left out for work; he had a lot of paperwork to do, so it was easy for her to get out without questions. I'm really happy my grandma's here. Paul seems to be happy too. They seem to be getting along well.

'Today's the day for Simon to get moved to the clinic, only he doesn't know that. I haven't seen him yet so I don't know how he is. Probably the same as he always is I suppose. At least today is the last day.

'As soon as grandma arrived she made it clear that we only had a few hours to put our plans together in getting Simon to submit - luckily dad is there (at the house; day off) so he won't miss anything. I still don't know how it's going to happen: exposing the truth and fears, and getting Simon to go with us all to the clinic; he's been pretty aggressive recently, I don't know how to handle that.

'Grandma, Paul and I left at 1pm. We decided to let things flow impromptu, besides, we don't really have the time to plan this out; we all have to leave today. Paul and I are finally leaving and we can't miss our train. We're going to get a train from London (after dropping Simon off) to Oxford - we want to make sure he gets there. I only hope that things work out.

'Mum and dad were at the house when we got there. I turned the key and walked in followed by Paul - whom they had barely seen before, and Grandma. That was a shock. Mum opened up her eyes really wide, mouth opened, and dad ... he had a mixture of shock and joy written over his face as he went to hug her. It was quite touching watching them embrace but it wasn't for long. Dad started to ask questions but we were more interested in getting Simon. Then he started to ask questions about

EVERYONE'S PERSPECTIVE

that. "Why were we in such a hurry?", "What was wrong with Simon?", "Where were we all going?" (Mine and Paul's luggage were showing). Obviously we had no choice but to explain the whole situation.

'I told dad of our first suspicions of Simon when he started to act weird and detached. Of our suspicions of drugs - dad never believed it, but then I told him of how we found the drugs, how I used to see Simon on one of his many trips, how he started to deteriorate, withdraw - and how now he's even more distant than ever, even irritable. I watched dad's face change through a range of emotions; shock, pity, anger, sorrow. He asked me why I didn't do anything, and I told him that I did. That's why we were here. That's why grandma was here. He turned to mum and began to ask her why she didn't do anything. How come she never knew of this? How could she have missed it? Mum looked blank. Speechless. She couldn't find the words quick enough and we were all staring at her. Her mouth opened and closed. She looked back from one pair of eyes to the other until she had seen us all. No words came out of her mouth. She looked pitiful. I couldn't stand looking at her. I started filling in the blanks.

'I spoke of her raiding my room - she was shocked at that, I was happy. I spoke of her constant ignorance of Simon; how she'd ignore him when he walked in the room when he said "hello". When he looked at her. I spoke of the filthy looks she would shoot at him, how she'd mutter about him when she thought no-one was listening, and how, after every trip that Simon had, even when it was pretty conspicuous to see or hear, she'd pretend that nothing was happening because she hated him. Grandma listened in quiet fury but dad ... he looked like he was going to explode. His face was becoming so red. Mum didn't say anything but she stopped looking at us all though. I spoke of her frequent dinner parties of old and new when dad was away. Her constant need to flatter the neighbours instead of looking after her own son.

'I left my father with that information and went upstairs with Paul to get Simon. We could hear dad explode; him shouting at mum asking her

EVERYONE'S PERSPECTIVE

"Why?", her shouting back. Grandma still remained silent. Simon had heard the whole conversation from downstairs. As soon as we walked through the door he asked me, all sad and pathetic, how we knew. He thought no-one else knew. And why didn't I help him? I told him I was helping him now. He looked so small as the tears rolled down his face. So much like a boy. He didn't need submitting; he had already given up. My poor helpless brother surrendered.'

Suzie on Charles Eliot:

'Eleanor has not been around recently. Her things are gone and she's sometimes nowhere to be found. All my wiles to get her to stay and to find out what she's up to have failed. It has just been an empty house with just me and Simon. Then all of a sudden Eleanor shows up and not alone either. She shows up, bags in hand with this boy, and her grandmother. I haven't seen that woman since Charlie and I were in college together. I was shocked to say the least.

'Eleanor has always been my favourite but somehow that girl has changed. The way she looked at me when she entered the house: no smile, no pleasure, just pure disgust. She started to tell her father everything. All these things I never thought that she knew about me. I was so ashamed. I couldn't believe it. She knew about me searching her room. She knew about my feelings towards her brother. I always knew he was going to bring trouble into this house. And now look.

'She picked a good day to tell all this: when her father was around. I couldn't talk my way out of it. There was nothing I could do. They were all staring at me. Judging me. They all knew. Charlie was the worst though. I thought the look that Eleanor gave me was bad. But this! ... Oh God! It was horrible. He was just shocked and angry. He looked as though he hated me. Simon started taking drugs and all of a sudden it was my fault. Our argument was brutal. His mother stayed quiet in her cold contempt. She has never liked me. But they don't understand!

EVERYONE'S PERSPECTIVE

'Charlie kept pushing me and pushing me for answers. Laying down all the blame. Saying he thought he could trust me. How could I let this happen? I had no choice ... He just kept pushing me and it was bound to come out. So I told him why I hated his precious son. Every time I look at Simon I see his father. In every smile, in every gaze. His face just swims around behind Simon's eyes. People say I look like Simon, or Simon looks like me but when I look at him I see his father. That good-for-nothing brute! Charlie didn't understand. So I carried on.

'When we first moved here and I was struggling with going to university and working at the restaurant, the boss got a little bit friendly, knew I needed the money and offered to pay me more money if I could work on later shifts. I was happy. I thought it would be brilliant so I agreed. But, or course, there was a catch. Like I said, he was a bit "friendly", would get a bit touchy feely. Said if I did him favours he would make it worth my while. I was young and naïve and vulnerable, and I needed the money and the job.

'We started having an affair. He was married and I had Charlie. I wasn't proud of myself. The affair lasted for almost a year until I fell pregnant with Simon. I told him and he said he never wanted kids; him and his wife didn't have children and I should have an abortion. I refused and he fired me. I didn't know how I was going to tell Charlie and left it for two months until I was rushed to hospital. The doctor told me I was pregnant, no surprise, but that it was two babies not one, and that one was bigger than the other - two months, and the other was just recent. I never told Charlie. Told him it was twins and left it at that.

'I had Simon and Eleanor just minutes apart. Eleanor was premature. She was not Simon's twin, just his half-sister. I thought I might have been able to handle it. Treat Simon and pass him of as Charlie's, but the moment they put him in my arms and I looked at him, I saw his father.

'Charlie and his mother stood there looking at me. Charlie was full of loathing. He called me a dirty whore. Said how could I do that to him. I didn't know what to say. Simon is not his son and not his mother's

EVERYONE'S PERSPECTIVE

grandchild, only Eleanor is. Eleanor, Simon and the other guy heard everything. Now everybody knows the truth. So many faces full of disgust. They took Simon and left but not before Charlie said that we were over. He'd be filing for divorce. I was left all alone in the empty house. Everything crumbling around me.'

Charles Eliot:

'I thought I knew my wife, but now I find out I don't really know anything. It seems as though my whole life so far has been a waste. A lie. Full of deception. I just don't know anymore. My wife is not what I thought she was. My son is not my son. I left my father's home, my mother's love. I left a business and a lifestyle that I could have had success with for her! And all the while she's been lying to me. Betrayed me. I gave up everything for her. I don't know what to think.

'Simon has been wasting away under my nose and I wasn't there to protect him. I wasn't there to see it. I left him and his sister in their mother's care thinking she was a good mother. A kind and caring individual. I let him down. I let them both down. There's nothing left for Suzie and I. Our relationship is over.

'My mother, Eleanor, Paul and I left with Simon to take a train to London to the clinic. Simon didn't even fight. He followed us through the door of his old home and on to the train. He never made a sound, made a movement. Just sat there in perfect quietude. Things have changed so much and so quickly. He doesn't even look like the same person anymore. My mother assured me that it was a very good clinic and neither one of us have anything to worry about. He'll be in good hands. It's been really good seeing my mother again. I'm glad that she's here.

'When we arrived at the clinic Simon remained submissive. It was almost as though this was what he wanted. There was already someone there to meet him. A friendly looking woman in a white uniform shirt

EVERYONE'S PERSPECTIVE

top and trousers. She greeted us all. Smiled throughout and took Simon through to his room: we weren't allowed to follow so we all said our goodbyes before they went. We all gave Simon a hug: Eleanor crying and clinging to him fiercely. It looked really hard for her to let go, but she managed to in the end.

'Simon looked at us all in turn, his face impassive and his eyes lost. He allowed us to hug him but he never said a word, just turned with the woman - who had remained patient throughout - and left. Eleanor said her and Paul would be leaving soon. Explained their whole plan to me, said it was something she had to do. There's nothing I can do now; she's eighteen. I told her I hoped she'll be very happy, and that Paul looked like a nice bloke. Already, I have lost a wife and two children. I never expected this to happen. I'm going back with mother to her home, try to make things up with dad. I'm going to try and get myself a flat so that when Simon is better he'll have somewhere to live. To start over again.'

Eleanor Eliot:

'Paul and I left for Oxford soon after dropping off Simon. I'm glad he's finally gotten the help he needs but I'm sad about the whole departure. The family's all split up now and mum has been left all alone. I don't think I want to see her yet. I don't think I can. Dad doesn't want anything to do with her and right now I can't really blame him.

'Paul, as promised, got a job working with his uncle as a mechanic part-time, and I got a job part-time in a shoe store. The money's really good and Paul and I managed to get a flat together, still renting of course, but it's better than staying I part-time accommodations.

'We both started uni at the same time and because we go to the same university, we get to see each other the majority of the time. We spend some of our breaks together unless we have extra studying to do or work. Grandma and dad come up to see us sometimes and I go down to see them. We go and visit Simon together when we have time, and he

EVERYONE'S PERSPECTIVE

looks a lot better. He's making progress and is almost ready to leave the clinic. The counsellor said he's really opened up and even told them who he was getting his drugs from (it was a low life junkie student at school). He's even booked him in to retake his exams when he's better and studied more to get back on track. Everyone's really proud of Simon and we couldn't want anything more. We've all moved on and have started afresh and are getting along with our lives.'

Printed in the United States
By Bookmasters